DEDICATION

To Mom, Dad, Doug, David, and Anne, for loving book one; to Jess for continuing to draw like a rock star; to Jim for helping me carry whatever boxes I bring into our life together; to the First Friday crew for always being excited about my dreams; and to every student or teacher who visits B249 and touches my world.

www.mascotbooks.com

For more information, please contact:
Mascot Books
620 Herndon Parkway #320
Herndon, VA 20170
info@mascotbooks.com

Library of Congress Control Number: 2020915172

CPSIA Code: PRT0920A
ISBN-13: 978-1-64543-720-8

Printed in the United States

IMPERFECTPHIL IS WHO I AM!

Sue Steinhardt

Illustrated by Jessica Murr

I'm a dog. I'm a big dog.

A big, black and white dog who drools.

A big, black and white dog who drools
and has gigantic feet with tufts of hair
sticking out between my toes...

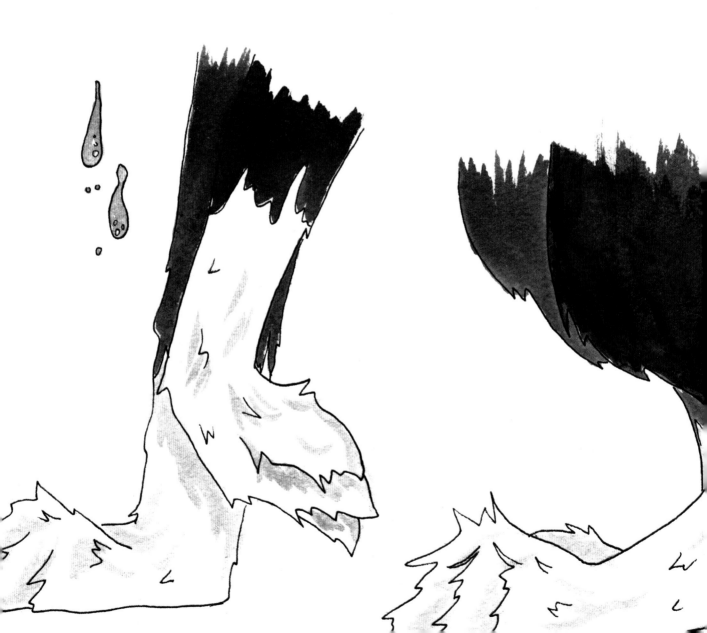

...and different colored fur all around my ears that kind of makes me look like I am wearing a wig.

People are naturally drawn to me. In fact, it sometimes takes longer than it should for us to go on a walk because so many people stop to say hello.

I love it when people say hello to me,
but I have noticed that they always
start the conversation by asking,
"What is he?"

I'm a dog. I'm a big dog.
A big, black and white...
well, you remember.

All of those people asking
"what I am" got me thinking...

While we were out walking the
other day, I looked around and
saw a bunch of dogs.

Some of the dogs were little brown dogs with long noses and short legs.

Some of the dogs were
medium-sized white dogs with
black spots and long skinny tails.

Some of the dogs were fluffy dogs with
lots of fur and eyes I could barely see.

Some of the dogs were nervous dogs
with dry noses and shaky knees.

While we were out walking
the other day, I looked around.

I saw one hundred dogs.
They were ALL dogs,
but none of them looked like me.

Do any of them look like a dog you know?

When people ask Mom "what I am,"
she always answers with, "He's a
St. Bernard and Mastiff mix."

So clearly, THAT is what I am.

what IS that?

According to what it says online,
St. Bernards are "calm, patient, and
gentle" while Mastiffs are "dignified,
loving, and affectionate."

I'm calm...sometimes.

I'm patient...sometimes.

I'm gentle...usually.

I'm dignified...debatable.

I'm loving...absolutely.

I'm affectionate...does that mean
the same thing as loving?

What do those words look like in action?
What do those words mean I do?
What do those words mean I am?

what IS all of that?

The other day I got so excited when mom called my name that I came running—no, flying—off the hill behind my house.

I hit the porch at full speed, which
caused my legs to spiral out from under
me, and I slammed into a deck chair...

...which caused the deck chair to fall over and hit another chair which then fell over and landed on top of me.

Which caused everybody on the porch to laugh.

At me.

Imperfectphil.

Philip Theodore Basher.

Phil.

A St. Bernard/Mastiff mix.

Imperfectphil, calm and dignified,
said no person ever.

While I lay on the porch under the pile of chairs,
I thought about what I do and who I am.

I'm a dog. I'm a big dog.
A big, black and white dog who drools.

Who are you?

I'm a St. Bernard/Mastiff mix, and if
I look online, someone else will tell me
what that means.

But...maybe what it says about me
on the Internet is not always true.

I'm a dog, I love life, and I have flaws.
I'm perfect. Imperfect.
Just. Like. You.

ABOUT THE AUTHOR

Sue Steinhardt is a high school English teacher with the simple philosophy of "be." She grew up in Belvidere, New Jersey, and still lives nearby with her husband and furbabies. Sue loves walking in the woods and sharing a laugh about the quirks of life with good friends. She loves dogs, believes in rescues, always recycles, drinks from a reusable straw, and tries to breathe deeply rather than act harshly. She is not perfect.

To stay in touch, follow her blog at imperfectphil.com. Check out Phil on Instagram @imperfect_phil, on Twitter @imperfectphil1, or send a friend request to Phil Basher on Facebook.

ABOUT THE ARTIST

Jessica Murr is a developing artist who learns as she goes. She hopes to spread her artwork around the world and make a positive impact. She grew up in Mount Olive, New Jersey, where she began her art career. There, she was able to grow and develop into the artist that she is today with the help of family, friends, teachers, and furry friends. Currently, she studies Visual Effects at Savannah College of Art and Design where she is always open to learning new things to make her life and those around her better.

To follow up on her journey through the art world, you can follow her on Instagram @jessilynneart.

Sue and Jess first met as teacher and student, and their journey to the *Imperfectphil* series is proof of how important those relationships can be.